A Madison's Imagination Story:

CHASING RAINBOWS

By V. L. Simer

TABLE OF CONTENTS

ACKNOWLEDGEMENT

To all of my friends and family who tirelessly read and reread this book while I wrote it, and were, what I called, my critical readers, I thank each and every one of you for your time and patience.

A very special thank you to my friend Kjester Buesig for taking the cover picture and for allowing me to share it.

DEDICATION

TO MADISON MARIE, my great-niece and the inspiration character of this story. Thank you for being my inspiration always.

At the time of this story, she is about 11-years old. Beyond the basic fact that I have a great-niece and she and her family inspired this story, it is purely a work of fiction from my own imagination.

It is my hope that all readers will be inspired by this story to seek out new lands and enjoy their culture. Also, that families will learn a little about how others function within their families and maybe find a little hint here and there that, hopefully, will help them along life's ever changing path.

Let your imagination go from time to time. It's good therapy.

V. L. Simer

CHAPTER 1

HMMMM - MADISON MUMBLED to herself, this room *really* needs something. She cupped her chin with her hand and squinting her eyes brought her dark eyebrows close together over her smoldering hazel-grey eyes thoughtfully. Probably a lot of something's she admitted - a major change in this room would definitely be nice. Turning slowly in a circle she carefully studied each of the walls and thought about what she was really seeing, not just looking but actually seeing. She saw plain walls painted a clean, creamy off-white with empty bright white painted shelves. Unlimited possibilities she thought. Like a blank piece of paper just waiting for the artist to create something beautiful with color and design features.

Knitting her eyebrows together with her mouth in a thoughtful frown and her lips puckered up and held tightly together, she considered how to make a positive and beautiful change to her bedroom. Madison seriously studied each wall as though it were an unpainted canvas waiting for her to take a thoughtful paintbrush of color and magically swipe it around the room and bring it to colorful life.

She looked at her bedroom furniture and thought it was neutral in appearance. The bed had a white headboard with a matching dresser with mirrored doors for clothes and a place to put the DVR with a shelf and chair underneath it. This was her place to do her homework. Above the homework shelf was the television mounted on the wall. Her room looked nice and clean and the best part, easy to decorate.

She focused on the window wall of the room and she thought about fairies. In a flash, she could see fairies in motion dancing around the window like a square picture frame in motion. There were little fairies dressed in clothes made from flowers with translucent wings fluttering faster than the eye could see. One was dressed in a pink tulip dress with a pointed hat from another tulip that had the stem part pointed upward on her head. Another had a beautiful lilac flower dress the next had a daffodil blossom for a dress that looked like two frilled skirts, one shorter than the other with a ruffled edge. There were dozens of fairies dressed in different flowers dancing and fluttering around the window in Madison's room. It seemed like every flower she had ever seen in all of the gardens in her neighborhood, and some that were new to her, had become clothing for the fairies. Madison smiled and as she did they turned and looked back at her smiling then waving at her. Madison couldn't stop herself from waving back at them and giggling. They were so cute. Who would think she could have real moving fairies around her window? What a concept.

Madison noticed the details; even the tiniest detail, and instinctively knew from her artistic perspective when each detail was important to complete the whole vision. She noted the fairies dressed in pink, blue, yellow, white or pastel colors had blond hair and fair skin. The fairies in the lilac and red flower dresses and other purple and greenish colors had reddish hair and lightly freckled skin. Others had dark brown hair like hers and their dresses were flowers in the darker colors of russet and scarlet, deep purple and blue and were both fair and tawny skinned. They all had tiny pointed ears, turned up noses, and were smiling as if they enjoyed moving around and around the window frame. They had many features that were similar, though each one had distinctly different coloring, face and figure. The most apparent trait of the fairies that was the same was their height; they were all about the same and only a few inches tall.

Turning toward the other two big walls in her room she visualized one of her favorite things in nature, a bright and beautifully colorful rainbow that arced from one corner of the big wall to the other with each individual color clearly showing in a blend of red, orange, yellow, green, blue, indigo, and violet. Then the rainbow got bigger and longer to extend around the room taking up two walls with the top of the rainbow arcing at the center corner of the wall up by the ceiling then continuing down to the wall and around the short corner to the bottom of the doorframe. Terrific, she said to herself. I love it!

Rainbows and fairies would be a good combination. I can decorate around that she thought excitedly.

Turning to another wall, the one by her study and television center, she detected a bit of movement in the rainbow and her eyes and head snapped back to look at the bottom corner of the doorframe. A very small pot of gold was there. That's interesting Madison thought, a rainbow with a pot of gold at the end of it. She smiled and thought that would be right; everyone knew there was supposed to be a pot of gold at the end of a rainbow. The hard part was figuring out which was the beginning and which was the end of the rainbow. Grinning she started to turn away again when her eye caught another slight movement by the pot of gold. Her head snapped back and she stared, the pot of gold was still there but nothing else. Oh well she considered, maybe it was nothing. She turned and was looking to the top arc of the rainbow. Again, she caught slight movement out of the corner of her eye, and immediately shot a look downward to the pot of gold where she saw the tiniest tip of a flat crowned little green hat peaking up from behind the pot of gold. Well - well, Madison wondered, what is this?

She leaned to the left as though she were turning around again and a tiny little head poked up from behind the pot of gold. Her head whipped around and she was looking eye to eye with a tiny little man all dressed in green. "Well, hello," Madison said to him, looking down and smiling.

Quick as a wink he dived back behind the pot of gold.

This is *very strange* Madison thought.   I thought about a rainbow and then my imagination took over, and I could see a pot of gold at the end of the rainbow with a shy little man all dressed in green.   Since the whole thing was against the flat wall she couldn't very well reach behind the pot of gold and pull the little man out of there, now could she? Just to test it she touched the wall and sure enough, it was as hard and solid as it had ever been and she knew she could not reach into it.

Sitting down on the floor, Madison studied the pot of gold at eye level.   Maybe if I just sit here very still and don't scare him, the little man will come out again and we can make friends or at least talk.   Madison once again let her imagination run on its own in hopes of conjuring the little man; but no, he did not pop up again.   What do they call those little men dressed in green that are by the pot of gold at the end of the rainbow? Hmmmm, she thought. I know the word.   Oh, of course, silly me it's Leprechaun. Yes, a Leprechaun. Why is there a Leprechaun in my room hiding from me? I'll watch for him to come back.

Soon she tired of sitting on the floor staring at the wall by the door and lay down on the soft carpet continuing to stare. She knew she could not take her eyes off the rainbow or the pot of gold or they might disappear with the little man dressed all in green. Maybe not, but maybe yes, and she did not want that. Now she was really curious.

Soon she was fast asleep.

CHAPTER 2

MADISON'S EYES SNAPPED OPEN and she was in a big place with bright clear blue skies and a long carpet-like covering of short, soft mossy green grass and colorful flowers growing wild. The ground looked as though it were carpeted in a green velvet fabric that fit snuggly over every flat and undulating hill over every portion of the ground around her and off into the distance changing from one green color to another as far as the eye could see. There was every color of flower, some very small and close to the ground in colorful clusters and others very tall and as big as a person's head. Others were somewhere between in height and the colors were bright and dark and light and pale, gorgeous pristine, perfect flowers whose faces looked upward toward the sun.

Glancing around her she thought every flower ever grown had to be found somewhere in the beautiful green grasses as far across the field as one could see in front of her. There were dozens of colors of green across the meadow in the velvet like carpet. Dark and light, bright and soft, some of the greens seemed to have a brown or yellowish tinge and others a yellow, blue or gray. Trees, bushes and shrubbery were scattered around the hillsides. Sometimes just one and in other areas, there were many of all different shapes, types and sizes grouped together.

Then she saw butterflies flitting from flower to flower. Every time they went to a different colored flower the butterfly would shimmer and shake then its delicate wings would change into the flowers colors. It was an incredible sight to see. She knew the butterflies by her house always stayed the same color no matter what color the flower they were drinking nectar from was. Is this magic, she wondered? There must be bees or other insects near the flowers also, because she heard a low sound of buzzing. Madison appreciated this strange and beautiful place.

Suddenly different sized and colored butterflies surrounded her. They seemed to fly and dance around her head like a wreath. She started to giggle and sat down to watch them. Each one was distinctively different in color, size and shape. Some were very tiny and seemed much too small to be able to fly. Some were large and had a variety of shapes to their wings with intricate designs. She could feel the flutter of air as they passed her in their flight.

She could identify the flowers they had been getting nectar from because their wings had changed to that color. It amazed her that the butterflies that had been to flowers of more than one color had all of those colors on their wings. A yellow daisy flower had a deep orange center that got lighter and lighter until it was a pale yellow on the outer edge. The butterflies that had enjoyed the nectar were colored orange near their body and light yellow at the furthest edges of their wings. The purple flowers with white centers were matched in the wings of the butterflies that had been there also. The same happened with the variety of colors and types of flowers throughout the meadow. They seemed so happy to just be flying around her and sharing the beauty of their colorful dance with each other, twisting and turning in the air. She felt very special to be included in this colorful showing.

Slowly a wreath of butterflies descended down to surround her face. As they passed, their wings lightly brushed her cheeks. Madison giggled and remembered her mother blinking her eyelashes very fast while snuggling her face. Her mother said those were butterfly kisses. Madison knew her mother would be surprised when she told her the eyelash kisses *did* feel like the butterflies kisses she was experiencing right then.

She could see the fields go on and on into the distance sometimes ending in craggy grey, red and brown sharp rocky ledges. There were miles and miles of low rolling hills that never became more than a mound by her estimation. Then there were a few tall mountains jutting up out of the ground. Strange, she thought, since her home was in a place surrounded by the very tall, tree covered Sierra Nevada Mountains. Her family lived in the valley below them. Every place was different. Every place has its own beauty.

There were dark gray clouds in the distance that looked as if they were raining straight down onto the hills below. I guess it has to rain here, she thought confidently, or the grass and flowers would not grow and stay green. I hope that cloud doesn't come this way and get me all wet. Looking around she saw no immediate shelter to protect her if the clouds did come toward her.

Behind her, the sun shined a clear bright light at the raining cloud and there in front of the cloud appeared the most beautiful rainbow Madison had ever seen. Each color in the rainbow was as sharp and clear as a color crayon. She watched in amazement. She could see the beginning of the rainbow on the left and the beginning of the rainbow on the right with the completed arc in the middle. I wonder if I have ever seen a complete rainbow outside of a coloring book or a photograph. I don't think so she admitted. Usually rainbows look like they fade out a little somewhere, or disappear at the top or on the sides. Sometimes there are two partial rainbows either side by side or one on top of the other. I wonder if there are ever three rainbows or more than that even. Wow, she thought, that would be great to see. Imagine a whole sky filled with rainbows. I want to be there if that ever happens, Madison admitted smiling.

Turning back toward the raincloud she saw the light brighten a little more and a second rainbow shined above the first one. Oh my goodness, Madison thought. A double rainbow - That is so totally cool. No, totally awesome. I wish I had a camera so I could take a picture. I would love to show this to my family. My Mom would love this she thought. My Aunt Ginny would especially love it because she takes pictures of rainbows whenever she sees them. Aunt Ginny says the eye of a camera could never completely capture the beauty of a scene as well as the human eye. And, when you see something it is always in your mind and you can recapture the image from your imagination anytime to enjoy. Madison knew that she would always remember this rainbow for sure.

Standing there, Madison realized the cloud had moved toward her a little and was not so far away. I might as well walk toward the rainbow and see if I can figure out which side is the beginning and which side is the end, since, for the first time, I can clearly see both ends. If I can figure that out, maybe I can find a pot of gold.

Wouldn't that be something? Her parents and sisters would be shocked if she found a *real* pot of gold, not like the flat one on her bedroom wall. Giggling to herself, Madison set out a little faster skipping and dancing sometimes doing a cartwheel or a flip heading toward the bottom of the right side of the rainbow. This is great she thought happily racing through the grass and flowers.

As she neared the rainbow, the colors seemed to fade and get lighter. I wonder why that is happening, Madison wondered as she walked. The rainbow was really clear further away but now, not so much.

It seems to me that, as a person would get closer to a rainbow it should brighten and you should be able to see the pot of gold more clearly. After a while, she thought, I should be near the end of the rainbow, and then she turned to look back where she had started. She could clearly see the grass was mashed down where she had moved through it. It almost looked as though the grass lay down in a path for her, in case she needed to find her way back to where she started. It was comforting knowing she could go back any time; back to the butterflies and flowers.

At the bottom of one of the rolling hills, Madison noticed craggy rough old dark brown and grey tree trunks with not many leaves on the branches. They looked like they had died a long time before or were in the process of dying. There were sparse little patches of grass and flowers at base of the trunks of the trees and clumps between them. Behind the trees was a glow. O.M.G. - Madison thought hopefully; it must be a pot of gold making that glow. I knew it! I just knew it!

Walking quickly but quietly on her tiptoes Madison sneaked her way down to the edge of the trees. She stood behind a particularly large tree trunk and thought; I probably blend with the trees pretty well with my long brown hair, hazel-grey eyes, brown pants, and brown top and sneakers. She was glad she was not wearing the shoes that flashed a light with every step; cannot wear those to sneak up on anything. Holding her breath then letting it out slowly she carefully peered around the right side of the tree trunk through the underbrush toward the glow.

The glow came from something in the middle of a cleared area beyond the tree line. She still could not tell exactly where it came from, but there was a definite yellow glow, a light of some kind. Like a fire but the color of the glow was yellow not red and was steady not flickering like a fire light. Practically she pondered, what could give off a bright steady yellow glow except a pot of gold? A yellow light bulb would, she corrected herself practically. But there are no houses out here. Looking out across the hills, she saw no sign of power poles power lines or any way she was familiar with for electricity to be carried from one point to another. She discounted the idea of a light bulb right away, that can't be the reason for the light. It must be the real pot of gold she thought convincingly to herself. That is one big pot, she thought excitedly, to glow that brightly. Oh, *I have got* to see this, she admitted excitedly.

Soundlessly she slowly moved from tree trunk to tree trunk getting closer and closer to the glow. Hiding from she knew not what, she moved steadily toward her goal, and the source of that yellow glow.

The glow brightened more and more as she neared it. Finally, she was behind the tree trunk nearest to where she thought the pot of gold surely must be found. Slowly and quietly, she peered around the trunk at the glow, and then quickly moved back behind it to think about what she had seen. Her heart was beating hard and fast. She thought if anyone had been near her, they would probably hear the pounding; and, she had forgotten to breathe again. Releasing her breath out slowly and quietly she calmed herself.

She took slow deep breaths as she replayed what she had seen in her mind. In the middle of the clearing she had seen what looked like a large, old round brown rusted metal pot, which sat on fat little legs that kept it off the ground. She could not remember exactly what she saw on the top. She thought the pot stood above the dirt and the glow came up out of the top. She would have to sneak a peek again.

With her heart pounding, she squatted down, moved her hair away from her face, held her breath and peered around the tree trunk to the other side through the grasses and vines. Though her intent was to quickly look, she stopped to really look and study the sight. Yes, she was right; there *was* a big pot in the middle of the clearing. Yes, there was a bright yellow glow coming from the top. The glow seemed to get brighter and brighter as she stared. She started to move around the tree when she caught a glimpse of something moving near the pot. She froze, letting her breath out slowly.

Peeking over a low lying branch through the sparse leaves and through some tufts of green and gold grasses, she saw a little man about the size of a child; only a few feet tall. She knew he was a man and not a child by the beard on his chin. He looked like the little man she had seen behind the pot of gold on the wall in her bedroom at home.

He was dressed all in green with a dark green flat-topped hat cocked a little crookedly to the side on his head. He wore a short dark green jacket with tails in the back and a light green vest with seven golden buttons in two rows. He had short dark green pants that only reached his knees with a shiny gold buckle, which fastened a black belt around his round belly. His legs were covered with green and white striped socks that formed circles around his legs and went from his knees down to his buckled black shoes that had tipped up pointy toes. What an odd way to dress she thought?

His head was big; way too big, for his height and round little body she thought. He had round rosy cheeks and a red beard that went from ear to ear around his chin but had no mustache. His ears were large and pointed at the tops making him seem very alert behind the tiny glasses propped on his nose. He looks a little like the fairies, she realized, only much bigger than fairies. The animated story fairies, she knew, were tiny, only a few inches tall and cute, with pointed ears and wings on their backs. They were really little. He was bigger and didn't look like he had any wings; or, none she could see anyway. Oh my goodness, maybe he is some kind of large wingless fairy. She tried again to remember what she knew about Leprechauns and little men dressed in green by a pot of gold.

CHAPTER 3

I BELIEVE HE MAY BE a Leprechaun, Madison thought congratulating herself. She thought back to a story she had read about the folklore surrounding leprechauns. She remembered they were supposed to be mischievous little people who made shoes, did magic and saved money in a big pot of gold. Oh my - could this little man truly be a leprechaun or was he just a short person? She wouldn't want to insult him by thinking of him as a leprechaun when he might just be a "little person." Why would he be dressed in green in front of a big pot if he weren't a leprechaun? How silly, of course he's a leprechaun! What could be inside a big pot glowing yellow with a leprechaun near it if it didn't have any gold in it? A lot of questions she admitted, but she had no answers – not yet anyway.

She continued to watch, unseen by the little man, as he went about his work. He kept going behind the big pot to get things then brought them around to the side of the pot she was nearest. There was a stool with a wooden thing on a post at the front that kind of looked like a small horse's head turned backward. Again he disappeared behind the pot and came back with a table. She could tell the table was heavy for him because the little man leaned way back and his face turned red when he carried it. Then with a whoosh, he dropped it by the stool. Wiping his face with a little green handkerchief he pulled from a front pocket the man straightened his hat crookedly and again went back behind the pot.

What is he going to do with those things Madison wondered? Pretty soon he came back but this time he had a long belt with tools hanging from it. He put the belt over the backward horses' head on the stool and disappeared behind the pot again. A few seconds later he was back with a big dark brown piece of what looked a little like a kind of heavy fabric but might be leather. He wrapped the tool belt around his waist fastening the buckle. He drew a knife from the belt and moved the heavy fabric onto the table top. Concentrating intently, he looked over the top of the glasses balanced on his nose. He took measure of the fabric and drew a deep line across it with the knife. Then he held up the piece he had cut out. He seemed to be satisfied with what he saw and cut more in different shapes. What is he making, Madison, the unseen observer, wondered?

He went about his work with little notice of the world around him concentrating carefully on the tasks at hand. I'll bet he is cutting out shoes, Madison figured thoughtfully, as she again remembered the story she read. He's probably making shoes. They must be for a child because they are very small. How nice she thought, that this man would make something for a little child. He must be a very kindhearted man.

She calmed and her heart returned to a normal pace as she settled herself down to quietly watch. She felt safe and comfortable at the bottom of her tree watching the little man go about his work. He cut out more pieces then put them on the backward horse's head moving them around until they were in the position he wanted. He threaded a needle and began efficiently sewing the pieces together.

First he worked on what had to be the bottoms then he sewed on the sides. He took another tool, a pointed one, with a long shaft and wooden handle then reached for the hammer looped in his belt. He laid the shoe on its side on the table and hit the wooden handle on the back of the pointy tool with the hammer driving the pointy tool into the fabric. Then he wiggled it back and forth to remove the tool. Oh, I get it, holes for the shoe laces Madison thought.

He continued up one side and down the other making sure the holes were straight across from each other. That has to be right. After he finished one shoe he did the same things on another; and when he was done he had two, then three, then four and by the time the efficient little man was through he had cut and sewn twelve pair of small shoes one pair slightly larger than the next. Who does that?

Madison wondered. Who makes twelve pair of shoes for little children? Wait – maybe he has twelve children and is making shoes for them. Maybe, she thought.

Without warning, Madison sneezed. It was one of those surprise, sneak up on you sneezes, hard and loud enough to make you shiver all over. She didn't even have time to quiet the noise by covering her mouth. When she recovered she realized she had, unknowingly, rolled out from behind the tree trunk and was in clear view of the little man. Quick as she had ever moved, she scrambled back behind her tree trunk and sat with her back stiffly pressed against the bark holding her breath. She tried to blend into the rough gnarly bark. What would he do to her? Oh No!!! This is the worst thing ever. What if he meant to harm her? He had a hammer and a pointy thing. What if – she didn't even know what if? She wished she could melt inside the tree where she could not be seen or found. This could be bad, Madison thought, but wasn't sure what bad would be in circumstances like this.

Madison continued to press herself against the tree uncontrollably shaking. Should I run away she thought. No, if I run he will really be able to see me. I am staying right here. Maybe he didn't see where I went when I got back behind the tree.

Gradually she relaxed some and tuned in to the sounds around her. She could hear the underlying buzz of the bees and insects. She could hear and feel a light breeze moving across the grass and through the trees. Off in the distance she heard the tinkling sound of running water in a small creek. She heard birds chirping away in the trees. She could smell the fresh clean grasses with a touch of the sweet scent of flowers. What she didn't hear was the sound of a small man making shoes on the other side of the tree. There were no tapping sounds from the hammer and there were no sounds of thread being drawn through fabric to sew the shoes. Had the little man run away? Was he even there?

Gathering her courage Madison cautiously peeked around the tree on the side opposite the one she had rolled out from behind. She moved the grass and flowering plants aside so she could peek out at the pot. The pot was still there and it still had the glow. The table, bench and tools were still in place and the twelve pair of little shoes remained side by side on the table. What was missing was the little man who made the shoes. Where had he gone? Did she scare him away? Where was he? Would he come back?

CHAPTER 4

SLOWLY AND CAUTIOUSLY, Madison stood up and stepped around the tree trunk keeping her hands on the tree in case she had to dash back behind it. Carefully she looked in all directions and realized the little man had certainly vanished. She took one step toward the pot of gold and then another, she stayed ready to race back behind the tree if need be. Step followed careful step toward the big pot. As she drew closer she got more excited to see what was inside. Nearing the pot, she realized it was much taller than she had thought from her hiding place on the ground behind the tree. When she was right beside it she knew no matter how much she stretched and stood on her tip-toes she would not be able to see over the top edge of the pot. Even though she was much taller than the little man she was still too short to see over the edge of the pot. She tried jumping up with her arms extended to catch the edge and pull herself up. But try as she might she could not reach.

What am I going to do Madison pondered? I know, I'll drag the table over, then climb up and see what's inside. Grabbing hold of the edge of the table closest to the pot Madison pulled and pulled trying to get it to move closer to the pot. She could not make the table move. She sat on the ground with her back to the table and tried to stand up and lift it with her back but it would not lift up even a little bit. When the little man dropped the table it must have sunk deeper into the ground than she thought. I knew it was heavy, Madison thought, and what am I going to do now? I really want to see what is in that pot. I want to know what is making the top of the pot glow so bright. It was obvious the stool the little man sat on to do his work was far too short to help her and she didn't even try to move it.

I've got it, she thought. Then she pulled herself up onto the table and stretched up on the very tips of her toes. She could just see the top edge of the pot but not over the edge down into the pot to what was inside. She was still too far away to jump and grab hold and pull herself up. This won't work she thought frustrated, and sat down cross legged on the table to think. It would be nice if eyes could see around corners and down into things. That would be strange she giggled, picturing herself with googely eyes that moved independently of each other like a lizard. Weird. Madison thought shaking her head to get rid of the mental picture of herself with lizard eyes. She did not want to go there.

CHAPTER 5

UNKNOWN TO MADISON while she was sitting on the table wondering how to reach high enough to see into the pot and grow googely eyes, the little man was watching her unobserved, from the top of the same tree trunk Madison had previously been hidden behind.

He hid himself carefully in the few branches and leaves in the top of the trunk of the tree the thing had hidden behind. Who is this he wondered? What is it? What does it want? It looks human, or what he imagined a human would look like, if he had ever seen one before; and he hadn't.

When he heard the explosion he just *"poofed"* and disappeared, landing on top of the tree. He knew it moved quickly behind the tree and stayed there for a long time. He just hid and felt like his fast beating heart would pound right out of his chest. He had been frightened it would hear him and do him harm. What was he going to do now? He knew it could be disastrous if it caught him. That must never happen. Stories had been told throughout the years about the incautious who allowed themselves to be captured. That frightened even the bravest of his kind.

Gathering his wits about him the little man studied the thing on his work table. It took up almost the whole table sitting on it. The table almost looked like a stool or step under it.

It had long brown hair that glistened with colors of gold, red and brown in the glowing light from the pot. Its face was pleasant with a small turned up nose and soft hazel grey eyes. It had a brown shirt and pants and brown things on its feet that didn't look anything like the shoes he made, so he thought maybe its feet looked like that on their own and it didn't need shoes. Its feet were very large compared to the shoes on the table. One thing was for certain, it wasn't like him.

CHAPTER 6

MADISON STOOD UP FROM THE TABLE; she decided she would go see what was behind the pot. She walked around it to the back side and was surprised to see nothing more than the back side of the pot, which looked pretty much like the front. She continued on around and soon found herself in front of the pot again. Nothing had changed. The table and stool were still there and there were twelve pair of small shoes on the table right where they had been before she started her walk.

Curious, she wondered - if the little man was in fact a leprechaun, wasn't he supposed to protect the pot of gold from people? How could he protect it if he wasn't even there? Was he there? Maybe he's invisible, Madison hesitated, maybe he is right here but I cannot see him.

Madison squinted her eyes tightly and looked around carefully, studying the ground for anything that didn't look normal. The grass looked like grass. The flowers looked like flowers. The trees looked like trees. The sky was still blue and bright with soft white clouds slowly moving with the breeze. The rainbow was still in place though muted in color. No footprints showed up on the ground like someone unseen was walking around leaving a mark. Everything looked the same as it did before she sneezed. Something *was* different Madison could feel it, but simply couldn't identify it.

Maybe instead of studying things so hard I should just glance at them to see if anything is different. So as casually as she could she began looking around. She looked under the pot and saw the tree trunks and grasses on the other side. She looked under the table, then felt silly, because she was pretty certain if a little man dressed all in green with a top hat, had been under the table she would have noticed him before now. Nope - no little man to be found anywhere she confirmed.

She stood up and stretched as tall as she could and looked at the trees beyond the clearing. She didn't see anything moving that the breeze couldn't cause. She let her eyes move closer and closer to the clearing until she settled on the tree trunks closest to her and the pot. She walked around the pot and did the same from all sides looking around and underneath. What if the little man was magic and could make himself a part of the trees? She would never find him if he could do that.

Wait, – she thought. Maybe I need to talk calmly to him so he will come out. That's it – he is probably scared I'll hurt him. "Hello," Madison said quietly looking around, "please come out. I won't hurt you. I mean you no harm." Nothing. No little man appeared. "Please, I would just like to talk to you. My name is Madison."

What if he doesn't speak English, Madison pondered. Well that won't work because that's the only language I know. She tried to remember some of the Spanish her friend Yolanda had been trying to teach her and came up with nothing besides hola, which means hello, and gracias, which means thank you - big deal. Anyway weren't leprechauns from Ireland? Yes, she was sure they were from Ireland and Madison did not know a single word in Irish besides leprechaun; oh and shamrock, which was a plant that grew a four leafed clover if you were lucky enough to find one. Big help. Wait, she did know another word in Irish; Donagal, her mother's last name before she got married to her father. Whoopee she thought deflated; now she knew three Irish words and two Spanish words that would not help her at all. Then laughing out loud Madison found herself holding her sides. Silly-silly girl.

Slowly, she regained her composure. I have to figure this out Madison said. Where is that little man? I have many questions to ask him.

Watching from his safe perch in the top of the tree the little man watched it walk around the pot, looking far and wide, he suspected, for him. Then he was shocked when it began to speak in a calm quiet voice. He understood what it said;

leprechauns' have the gift of language. He could understand any language. In fact, he never really realized there were different languages in different places. Talk was just talk to him. He understood and could reply if he chose. Right then he did not choose to let it know he understood or could hear, especially since he was not sure what it was or what it wanted. It looked a little like him and his kind only lots bigger and way different.

He had always been right where he was. He had followed his father, and grandfather as the keeper of the pot. For as far back as could be remembered for thousands of years the eldest male in his family had the honor and distinction of guarding the pot. Secondarily they were there to make shoes. The shoes were picked up anonymously and given to people who needed them. In turn, pieces of gold were left in their place. The gold was then hidden inside the pot by the guardian and the process repeated itself throughout time.

He had to admit, though he was honored to be the guardian of the pot, he had wondered from time to time what was beyond the pot and his cobbler duties of making shoes. He knew he wasn't supposed to think of those things, but when you were tasked with doing the same job day after day, year after year, your mind was sure to wander and wonder. He knew everyone had a job to do and this one was his.

CHAPTER 7

MADISON TRIED AGAIN TO COMMUNICATE with the little man in hopes he was near enough to hear her. "Hello," she said a little louder, "Can you hear me? My name is Madison and I mean you no harm. Please come out and talk to me. I would like to know about your work and the big pot with the yellow glow." She waited patiently, but no answer. She thought; I'll just give him a minute. "I know you don't know me, but I won't hurt you," she stated, knowing it was the truth. "It scares me to think I am all alone," she admitted, "please come out and talk to me."

Looking around she realized what she said was the truth; she was a little bit frightened to be all alone.

Slowly a large tear escaped from her eye and trickled down to her chin. The tear of a frightened child, a magic source of power as no one could ever stop from comforting a child who was in need.

Clearly Madison heard, "What do you seek?" in a strong deep voice with an accent she could not name from a place she could not see. "What are you?"

What do I seek? And what am I? Madison wondered. Odd questions. I guess I should answer the voice she thought. "I seek to know about this big pot. And I am a girl," she said. Thinking he may need more specific information, she added, "a human girl."

A girl, a human girl. Well-well, the little man thought, I was right it is human. He congratulated himself; it is a human and a girl, just what he imagined. "From where do you come?"

"I come from America - the United States of America," Madison told the voice. "Can you come out so I can see you?" Madison asked looking carefully around for the source of the voice.

"No! You might explode again." The little man said with caution. "Who knows what you might do next?"

Smiling with a little giggle in her voice, Madison said looking in the direction she thought the voice came from, "I did not explode! I sneezed because I was hiding in the grass and flowers and it tickled my nose. Don't you ever sneeze when your nose gets tickled?"

"Well yes," the voice admitted, "I guess I have sneezed a time or two, but certainly not as loud as you. I was scared, err startled."

"Maybe it is because I am so much bigger than you that my sneeze was louder," Madison admitted thoughtfully.

"Maybe so," He considered. "I might be tempted to let you see me but you have to promise you won't hurt me or try to catch me in any way. If you do not keep your word, I will disappear and you will not see me again."

"I promise," Madison solemnly stated holding up her right hand and meaning it. She had no intention of harming the little man. She just wanted to understand about him and the pot. She was also curious about those little shoes.

Seeing movement her eyes shot to the top of the tree she had hidden behind. She saw the branches move and a head popped out. It was the head and face of the little man with a green top hat. Madison started talking fast in hopes the little man would not disappear before she could say everything that came into her head.

"Well, hello." She said smiling up at him. "I'm happy to actually see you. I'm not sure how I got here but I saw a beautiful rainbow then two, and followed the yellow glow, thinking it might be the pot of gold at the end of the rainbow, even though I wasn't sure which end was the beginning and which was the end. Then sure enough when I saw the yellow glow I knew I was right. A little later I saw you get your stool then this table and you began making shoes. What is it with these little shoes anyway? Do you have twelve children somewhere? If you don't, who is going to wear them?"

Taking a deep breath, she stopped rapid firing questions at the little man. Her mother always said she was full of questions and wanted the answers to all of them right at the second she asked. Her mother also said no one had all of the answers all of the time and sometimes she should give people a few minutes to think about things before they gave an answer, otherwise the answer she got may not be the best one.

Staring wide-eyed the little man listened to Madison firing questions at him. When she finally stopped he took a deep breath, and trying to remember all of the questions he replied, "I am not sure which side of the rainbow is the beginning and which is the end but I know that I am the guardian of that pot right there," the little man explained pointing. "I have always been here and have always made the shoes."

"Did someone teach you?" Madison queried.

"I learned from my father who said he learned it from his father and on and on as far back as time can be remembered and then some. We have always cobbled and guarded the pot. For your next question, no I do not have twelve children. I make the shoes and leave them on the table. The next day the shoes are gone and payment is left on the table. I take the payment and hide it just like I was taught." The little man thought this was probably the longest conversation he had ever had, and the only questions he had ever heard from a human. He had never been questioned about who and what he was before.

"Are you a leprechaun or a little person?" Madison asked directly.

"Ach, there is that word," the man said gruffly, "do I have to be a kind? Do I have to be a leprechaun or a little person; can't I just be a man?"

"Well no, I guess you don't have to be either one. You could just be shorter than me. How old are you?" She asked directly not following up on the leprechaun issue.

Pursing his lips to one side while squinting his eyes he thought, "I'm not quite sure how old I am, but many years that is for certain. Yes, I am many years old, I am.

If you must know a type of being, I am of the leprechaun type. There are also fairies, pixies and sprites here about. We sometimes get confused with gnomes but I can assure you I am *not* a gnome of any kind. And *never ever* confuse a leprechaun, fairy or sprite with a troll. That will get you into a lot of trouble around this place." He said shaking his head up and down in confirmation.

Trying to change the conversation a bit, and not wanting to upset him, Madison asked, "Where do you live? I don't see any houses in this grass or out there on the hills. I also don't see any others like you." Then thinking he might be the only one, and was instantly saddened to think it, she asked solemnly, "Are you the only one? Like you, I mean."

Chuckling a little the man said, "No-no. I am not alone in the world, if that is what you are asking. There are many others like me. Well, some are younger and some are older but we are of the same being. I am the only one here in this particular place, as it is my sole job to protect the pot and make shoes. The others have duties for which they are responsible that contribute to our community also. Everyone has something in particular to do and accomplish."

"You must get lonely," Madison said thoughtfully, "who do you talk to?"

"Right now I am talking to you."

"I know." She said a little exasperated, "but who else do you talk to? Do others come to see you? Do you ever get to leave this place?" Madison had, again, rapid fired the questions at the little man.

Pondering the questions, the little man said, "One day a year, at The Feast Day Festival, I hide the pot in a special magical place and we all gather in the meadow for a celebration. There is much singing and dancing and laughing. Fairies, pixies, sprites and leprechauns; others like me, and all of the animals, insects and birds in our area gather together to celebrate. We renew ourselves for the coming year and we are visited by the king and queen."

"You have a king and queen?" Madison asked excitedly, immediately interested, "Who are they?"

"Why everyone knows who the king and queen are," he said as though the question were ridiculous. "They are the most royal of all the fairies, pixies, sprites and leprechauns. They are King Jason and Queen Amanda. They are the most handsome and beautiful of beings. One day a year they spend the day with us and we are honored to be in their presence. We all wear our finest clothing and shine our newest shoes, and when the king and queen appear all beings bow and curtsey before them. Across the land as far as the eye can see beings of every type come to pay their respect and celebrate."

With a sigh of remembrance, he went on, "The King raises his golden scepter and announces, 'The Feast Day Festival shall commence,' which is followed by musicians playing music and hundreds of tables with every kind of food and drink imaginable. We eat, we drink, we dance and play, and we laugh, we visit with each other to share stories of the past year and renew our friendships. Oh yes, it is indeed, a great day of celebration. We eat, laugh, dance and sing from dawn to dawn for one whole day."

"What happens after that day?"

"We return to our daily tasks, of course. We each have responsibilities." The man explained with certainty, "We all have work to do and I have a pot to guard and shoes to make."

"It doesn't sound like you have much fun if you only get to have it for one day," Madison admitted. "I get to have fun of some kind every day."

"What is this fun?" The man questioned the word. "I do not know fun."

"What is fun? What is fun? Well it's like reading a story and laughing at the words, because you can imagine what is happening in the story and it is funny. Or making faces at your sisters that makes them laugh out loud so you laugh too. Or getting to do cartwheels or run in the grass on a sunny day at school. You could have fun just hanging out with your friends. Or, you could have a sleep over and have fun playing with toys at your house or at your friend's house. Watching a movie with your family is fun and you don't have to do anything then but listen and watch. We talk to each other in my house and we laugh and help each other and that is fun too. That is what fun is. Anything you say or do that makes you smile or makes you feel good inside like the way you must feel during The Feast Day Festival." Madison informed him.

"Sometimes fun is painting a picture of something you have seen or something you imagine. I imagined a rainbow and let it get bigger and bigger in my room and then a pot appeared and you showed up and I saw you. Then like magic, here I am. That's a kind of fun - well sort of like fun, or maybe more like the beginning of an adventure."

"I do not know these things," the little man admitted shaking his head, "but I am happy that you get to have your 'fun' in so many ways and every day too."

"Do you have a name? What do others call you?" Madison asked realizing she was just thinking of him as 'that little man' instead of by his name as is proper. "My name is Madison."

"Yes, Madison, I do have a name. My name in Amharach or Lucky."

"Lucky," Madison repeated trying the name on for the little man "Is it alright if I call you Lucky then?"

"Certainly you may call me Lucky, that is my name," he said smiling indulgently down at her. "May I call you Madison?"

"Of course you can call me Madison that is my name. But I have another name," she quickly added. "Sometimes my family calls me Mimi. It's a nickname my grandmother, I call her Nanny, gave me when I was very little. I'm not sure I know why she called me that but she did and I like it too. Mostly people other than my family, just call me Madison."

She looked up smiling at Lucky glad to know something more about him and happy to share information about herself with him. This was turning out to be a good experience she thought. "I guess you don't have a nickname because Lucky is a pretty short word on its own." "Do you know why they call you Lucky?" Madison asked.

"No, that is just the name I have always been known by. I do not know why – some things, like a name, just are, for no particular reason at all."

Madison thought about it for a minute and decided he was right. Some things just are, for no particular reason at all. She could agree with that.

"Where does your family live?" Madison asked in her quest to learn more about Lucky. I haven't seen any houses. Looking around she reassured herself there were definitely *no houses* on the hills that she could see.

Chuckling to himself, he said, "You won't see our houses anywhere. They are enchanted and are invisible to anyone but seers like me. We can see them but others, outsiders, cannot. My kind live in the mounds and hills and in the meadows, others live in the gardens and forests. Some live near waterways large and small. Some others live in the houses of the large people. I would think you might be one of the large people I have heard about. Maybe there are those who live in your home that you cannot see unless they allow it."

Thinking carefully, Madison remembered a movie she once watched about a family of tiny little people who lived in the cracks and crevices of a home. The little people would go into the house when no one was looking or at night and take tiny little bits and pieces of food and other things they needed from the big people who lived there. Could there be little people like that living in her house she wondered? Who knew? Before this experience she thought, the only real leprechauns were cartoons on the boxes of the cereal she ate at breakfast or on advertisements for St. Patrick's Day. Now here she was having a completely logical conversation with one. They were never going to believe this when she got back home.

"So tell me Lucky, am I right, did I really find the pot of gold?"

He began cautiously, "If you mean does that large pot behind you hold gold, I don't think I want to tell you that. You might think it was fine to take it from me. But you couldn't. It cannot be done. You cannot take it!"

Indignantly Madison huffed testily with her face turning red, "I wouldn't take it from you that would be stealing. I know better. I would never steal something. Do you know how much trouble I would get into if I stole something? My mother would put me in time-out for ten years for stealing. No! I would never take something that is not mine. That is called stealing and I do not steal!" Hurt and angry, she turned her face and body to the side, looking away from Lucky. Stealing, she thought feeling accused, I would not do that! I came looking for the pot of gold but not to steal it, just to see it and figure out which side was the end of the rainbow.

Thinking about what Lucky had said, she turned slowly to look directly at him with her piercing hazel eyes. "What do you mean I *could not* take it from you?"

"Well everyone knows you cannot *take* the pot of gold."

"How would someone get the pot of gold then?"

Without thinking Lucky said smartly, looking at Madison like she didn't know anything, "The pot of gold must be given, it cannot ever be taken. If someone tried to take it, it would simply vanish into thin air."

"Vanish into thin air," Madison mocked with disbelief, "Metal pots that big *do not* just vanish into thin air? That is not possible. Vanish - what a laugh." Giggling in disbelief she thought no way that big pot vanishes. "Okay, so how does someone have the pot of gold given to them?"

"Ah, that is the real question isn't it Madison?" he said cagily. "What *does one have to do* to have the pot of gold given to them as a gift? If I tell you that you might try it and then where would I be with no pot of gold to guard and no work to be done. I would cease to exist because I would have no purpose. All beings need purpose you know. No. I cannot let you trick me into telling you how to get the pot of gold." Lucky said adamantly. "I'm sorry but I just will not do that."

"Oh please," Madison pleaded earnestly turning to look right at him, "I promise, I will not try to take the pot of gold from you and give your life no purpose. That would just be mean and I am not a mean person. I would not harm you like that. Actually I would not harm you in any way."

Lucky thought Madison must be touched in the head if she thought he would trust her with the sacred secret of the gold. He wouldn't tell her that Leprechauns throughout time had been tricked into giving the secret away. He knew that he could not ever get close enough to her to let her catch him. He patted his pants pockets to make sure the leather pouches he always carried were deep down in his pockets so they would not fall out. In one pouch he had a silver shilling, a magical coin, which returned to the purse each time it was paid out so the carrier of the pouch was never without money. In the other he carried a few shiny gold coins he could use to try to bribe himself out of difficult situations. The gold coins looked more valuable than the silver but usually turned to leaves once he parted with them, tricking the would-be thief while the leprechaun vanished with the pot.

The true secret was; the person who wanted the pot of gold must never take their eyes off of the leprechaun. If they looked away he would disappear in a flash never to be seen again. *Poof* and the leprechaun would vanish. But if they kept their eyes on him and he offered the treasure of the pot of gold to them, and they took it; that person would know untold wealth forever. Lucky knew his primary task and greatest responsibility was to protect the pot of gold from anyone or anything that could or would take it from him.

CHAPTER 8

SUDDENLY THERE WAS A GREAT gust of wind from across the valley. Madison's long hair blew across her face so she couldn't see. She shook her head making her hair blow back and faced into the wind. What is this she wondered? This wind is pretty hard. Reaching back, she held on to the table to steady herself. The wind grew in intensity, and she had to really hold on tight to keep from being blown backward.

"Lucky, what is this wind all of a sudden?" Madison yelled above the howl. "Why is the wind blowing so hard?"

"I'm not sure" he yelled back grabbing hold of the nearest branches of the tree, "but hold on in case it gets worse."

And worse it got. The grass was blown almost flat. The flowers bent away from the wind and the loose leaves on the trees flew into the air spiraling upward. Madison didn't know what she would do if it didn't quit. She couldn't hold on forever.

Suddenly in front of the pot appeared a colorful fiery glow. Every color in the rainbow and many more seemed to swirl and shift as a being materialized from the ground up. The being was dressed in a long flowing robe that shimmered in changing colors.

As the wind slowed Madison recognized the form as a woman. She was fair of skin and had long brown hair braided and wrapped about her head with a long tail that had colored ribbons entwined in the braid flowing down her back nearly to the ground. On her head was a simple gold crown with a purple jewel in the center and red stones on either side. As she became clearer and clearer to Madison the wind stilled and the swirling colors slowed to a stop. The blowing leaves settled gently to the ground and all was quiet.

She was the most beautiful person Madison had ever seen, and she was only a few feet tall. Surprisingly Madison thought she looked like her mother only much, much smaller. She was more beautiful that any picture of any woman she had ever seen.

Lucky cleared his throat and whispered sharply down from the tree top. "Madison, you must curtsey."

"What do you mean curtsey?" Madison asked. "What is curtsey? Is it something you do? I do not know curtsey. Is it a dance or what?"

Exasperated he said, "Just bend your knees and bow your head, Madison. Hold your arms out to the side like you were holding the skirt of a dress and don't stand up or raise your head until she gives you permission."

"Oh." Madison said, remembering she had seen this in a movie. She got off of the table and bending her shaking knees, she curtsied and dropped her head to look at the ground and held her arms out to the side as though she were holding the skirts of a dress. It seemed a little silly since she wore pants, but who knew. "Why am I doing this? Who is she?" Madison asked Lucky in a whisper.

"She is the queen and you must show your respect. Now don't stand up again or speak again until she gives her permission."

Raising her arms gracefully above her head with her palms up the queen said in a clear strong voice, "You may rise."

Madison hesitated only for a second because her knees were shaking so hard she was afraid she would fall down. She stood up and raised her head to look eye to eye with the little queen.

"Hello, your highness" Madison said hesitantly, wondering if it was proper to speak before being spoken to so she waited before saying anything more.

"What is your name child?" the queen inquired then clarified, "By what name are you known?"

"My name is Madison. I am called Madison."

"Madison." The queen drew out carefully, "what a lovely name. What does it mean?"

"Madison?" Madison thought quickly, "I don't really know - it is the name of some cities in America. It was the last name of a president a long time ago. It is the name of a river in Montana. I don't think it especially means anything, it's just a name, a word my parents liked and named me."

"I see," The queen said. "Tell me why did you come here? What do you seek?"

"Those are the same questions Lucky asked me," Madison admitted honestly.

She took a deep breath and explained as fast as she could talk, glancing at Lucky to see his reaction. "Evidently, I am here because I was imagining how to change my bedroom at home. Then I imagined a beautiful rainbow on the walls that got bigger and bigger. Then I saw what looked like a pot of gold by my door. Then I saw something move. When I looked carefully I saw

Lucky's hat. I tried to reach him but it was part of the wall. I'm not sure how that happened or how any of this happened. I thought I needed to stare at the pot of gold so that I could talk to Lucky and maybe make friends with him; but I didn't know his name then. After a while I got tired and laid down on the floor, always keeping my eyes on the pot.

The next thing I knew I was here walking through the beautiful green fields with the colorful flowers growing. I saw the trees and the hills and watched the butterflies changing color and saw the flowers of every kind and color growing wild in the mossy grasses. Then I saw the rainstorm in the distance and the sun shining on the rain that turned into a double rainbow and I was curious to see if there was truly a pot of gold at the end of a rainbow. Of course, I wasn't sure if the left or the right side of the rainbow was the beginning or the end of the rainbow so I just headed this direction and at the end of my walk, here I am. So… am I in a lot of trouble? For being here I mean. I really do not need to be in trouble. I especially do not need to be in a lot of trouble." Madison took a deep breath realizing that she had done it again. She had shared a lot of information without breathing. She needed to learn to breathe and talk. She would have to work on that.

Throwing her head back the Queen laughed and laughed out loud clutching her hands to her chest. Her beautiful long hair nearly touched the ground. If it were possible she was even more beautiful when laughing than she was just standing and talking.

"You are precious, child," the queen graciously admitted in her lilting voice, regaining her composure. "I sense you have the most important qualities in the young. You are bright. You are curious. You have adventure in your heart. You are willing to learn, and I think in learning, you will be willing to teach others. I also see that you are fair of face and will someday be a very beautiful woman of your kind who knows the value in letting the young make discoveries on their own and grow from it. You see and appreciate beauty all around you and try to capture it in your art work to enjoy at the time and later in your mind. You are special Madison – very special indeed."

Looking up into the tree the queen said gently, "You may come down Lucky. No harm will come to you in my presence. Madison is no threat to you."

In a poof, Lucky went from the top of the tree to the ground in front of the queen where he bowed low removing his top hat, to show his respect and the bald crown of his head. He held his bow with his hat in his hand and an arm across his middle. "You too may rise Lucky. What have you learned from this child?" she asked him directly.

Clearing his throat Lucky reported to his queen, "Like you, I have seen and heard the qualities of curiosity and intelligence, with the many questions she has asked me. She has shown an interest in learning of our ways. She has stated she is honest and does not steal. She has followed the beauty of rainbows to this place and found the pot that I guard. She has shown herself to be honest by promising not to steal or try to steal the pot and rid me of my life's purpose. She has a comely face and a kind voice." Lucky admitted to his queen with the authority of one who has spent the most time with the stranger.

"I am glad to hear all of that and I agree." The queen stated. "What shall we do with you Madison?" She asked turning to face Madison directly.

"I don't know what you should do with me," Madison started, "but whatever it is I hope it is not painful or will get me into trouble."

Laughing again, the queen said, "We are a peaceful being and would never do you, or anyone else, harm. We seek to bring goodwill, help and beauty to the world. Without our kind the fields would not be green, the flowers could not bloom so colorfully, and rainbows could not catch your eye in wonder at their beautiful colors. No Madison, we mean you no harm. You are not of our world. While it has been a pleasure to meet you and speak with you, I am afraid you must go back to your rightful place. Your own home."

"I am sorry your highness, I don't mean to be rude, but I am not sure how I got here or why. I am also not sure how to get back home, to where I came from," Madison said in explanation realizing for the first time how true those words were. How did I get here? How am I going to get back home? "I think I have been gone for a long time now – my Mom, my mother, is going to be really worried or mad that I didn't tell her where I was going and when I would return. I wasn't aware that I was going anywhere so I'm not sure why or when I would have told her I was leaving."

"I will help you Madison," the queen declared earnestly, "but first I would like to give you a token of your adventure to our land." Reaching out her hand she nodded to Lucky.

At first Lucky turned his head away and acted like he didn't know what the queen wanted from him. She tucked her chin down and raised her eyebrows to let him know she meant it and stuck out her hand again. Reluctantly Lucky held out his hand and in it was a black pouch with three shiny gold coins. Hesitantly he handed them to the queen like they were his only ones or his favorite coins of all. Madison could tell he did not want to give them to the queen.

The queen turned to Madison and held out the coins to her. Madison reached out and took the coins. They were shiny gold and felt warm in her hand. She was instantly overcome with a feeling of joy and happiness. The air around her felt charged with electricity. She looked at the little queen and asked, "Will they turn to leaves?"

"No," the queen said smiling and chuckling, "these are given as a gift and will not turn to leaves or disappear. Only coins that are *taken* from beings like Lucky turn to leaves. The coins that are gifted to someone will last forever."

"Wait!" Madison exclaimed, "Why do I have three coins instead of one?"

"Always one more question with you Madison," the queen said smiling patiently, "there are three coins Madison so you may give the gift to your sisters also. You see I know that your sisters are Savannah and Brooklyn and the coins will be a token of their big sisters' adventure to our land, the land of the leprechauns, fairies, gnomes and sprites who give joy and happiness to a world seldom seen by your kind of being. Please share a coin with each of them when you get home and keep one for yourself to remember this time you have shared with us. Now lie down on the table here and let your mind drift. Soon you will be back in your own home."

"Can I ask one more question before I go?" queried Madison.

"Certainly," the Queen said. "What question do you have?"

"Well," Madison said, taking a deep breath and swallowing, "Lucky said that he only had fun for one day a year during The Feast Day Festival. I think it's sad that you only get to have fun for such a short amount of time. I wonder how you can have a whole year's worth of fun in one-day."

"I never thought about it that way." The Queen said thoughtfully. "We look forward to The Feast Day Festival all year. It did not seem like we were doing without anything the rest of the year. What are you trying to say to me, Madison?"

"What I mean is, where I live, we have fun all the time. Well not *all* of the time but regularly. We laugh at funny things. We say things to each other to make people laugh and we laugh too. We sing and dance. We read and watch movies. We spend time with our family and friends. Adults and children seek out ways to enjoy time alone and with each other. We have fun as often as possible. We look for fun and ways to make fun happen." Madison described to the curious Queen. "Can you understand what I am trying to tell you?"

Thoughtfully the Queen considered what Madison said. She began to walk around while she thought. I wonder, the Queen questioned to herself, are the people of this land being cheated out of the opportunity to have fun more often? Should we think about this awhile? "Maybe I should discuss it with the King." The queen looked up at Madison with a small thoughtful smile on her face. "Thank you Madison, for bringing this to my attention. I had never thought of this from a point of view like yours. No one has ever posed a question like that to me or my husband that I know about. I wish you could observe The Feast Day Festival celebration so you would see firsthand how happy and joyful our people are and realize it may be possible to have a year's worth of fun in a single day."

"I wish I could see it too Queen Amanda; but Lucky told me that this whole area is enchanted and that is why I can't even see who the other people are and where those people live." Madison admitted earnestly looking beyond the queen to the countryside behind her. "That would be one of the most wonderful experiences of my life."

"Let me think," The queen said turning away while cupping her chin with her hand in thought. She closed her eyes and seemed to become trancelike in thought. Slowly from the north the breeze began to get stronger and stronger until it was steady like the swirling wind that came before the queen had arrived. Soon Madison's hair was blown across her face causing her to close her eyes. She turned her face into the wind and her hair blew back nearly standing straight out behind her due to the winds speed. She shuttered her eyes with her hands so they wouldn't dry out, but she could still see.

Turning and swirling in the wind was a funnel cloud made up of dark colors that flashed like lightening and rotated from one bold color to another, as the funnel neared the place where they were standing the wind began to settle and slow its rotations. When it reached the place where the queen, Lucky and Madison waited, the cloudlike funnel began to clear. Starting from the bottom and moving up, they could see feet shod with shoes like the ones Lucky made with turned up toes and buckles, then blousy dark trousers tucked into the top of the boots, then a short jacket in patches of bold jeweled colors of purple, green, red, and blue satin and velvet. At the top a handsome man's face framed with wavy golden hair, caring blue eyes and a radiant smile with bright white teeth emerged. Then the wind stilled completely and the man stepped forward toward the queen.

"Welcome, my King," the Queen said smiling sweetly up at him. "I see you understood my request for your presence."

"Yes," said the King smiling down at her, kissing her lightly at the corner of her mouth, "our telepathic senses are working just fine today, my queen. Why have you summoned me? Though you needn't have any more reason than simply wanting to see me?" he gently teased.

Laughing the Queen took both of his hands in hers, "Of course I wish to see you my husband; however, I also need your assistance with a dilemma right now."

His eyebrows came together in a thoughtful frown, the king took her hands in his and said, "What is your dilemma and how can I help you?"

"First, I would like to introduce you to a visitor." Turning toward Madison, she held out her hand, and said, "This young one is called Madison. She is a human child who found herself here after imagining a rainbow in her room at home. Then she saw a pot of gold and the top of Lucky's hat peeking out from behind it. She said she lay down to keep her eye out for him and the next thing she knew she was here."

"Well, that is quite a story that seems to have become an adventure for you. It's a pleasure to meet you Madison," the king said extending his hand questioningly. "I am not sure how I can help you though. Do you wish to return to your homeland and do not know how to get back there? Have you been harmed in any way?" Looking carefully the king assured himself that Madison looked fine and unharmed to him.

Madison reached out her right hand to shake the King's hand and wondered if she should curtsey instead. It is too late now she thought, a handshake would have to do. "Your highness, I do wish to return home, but I would also like to better understand your people and The Feast Day Festival. As I have been discussing with the queen and Lucky I don't understand why you and your people only get to have fun for one day per year at

The Feast Day Festival. That doesn't seem like much fun to me. Where I live we have fun almost every day or at the very least we enjoy ourselves sometime every day."

"I see," the king pondered listening carefully, "culturally we must be very different." Turning to his wife the king asked, "Is the dilemma you referred to one of trying to figure out how to invite the uninvitable to our celebration, my queen?"

"You know me very well my King," she said sheepishly, "is it so wrong to want her to see the joy, spirit and love that we share with each other during our wonderful celebration? I feel she is a special gift that has been sent here to us and I feel it could be important for her to understand our ways. After seeing it firsthand she will know the joys we experience. It may be different from her own experiences where she lives, but valuable to her understanding of other cultures."

"What method of granting her participation in our celebration were you thinking about?" the king inquired. "We don't have many choices. Our people, along with the gnomes, fairies, sprites and pixies would be frightened to see someone like Madison at the festival. She is very large and if we shrunk her to our size, we already know we may not be able to restore her to her regular form."

Turning to look up at Madison the king explained earnestly, "We had a problem with that many centuries ago and the human was never able to return to their home because we could not restore them to their original size. That person remained with our people and had a fulfilling and purposeful life but we always knew they felt a bit cheated by not being able to return to their homeland."

Turning back to the Queen he said thoughtfully, "We could remove the enchantment of our region so that she could see what is happening, but if she can see it so can others who may wish to bring us harm. I am not certain what the most appropriate way to help her is."

"I know the difficulties of which you speak my husband," the queen said with caution, "but what if we made her part of something that already exists in our area that would place her in a position to see what goes on without any of our people knowing she's there?"

Walking in front of the cobbler's bench the queen thought aloud carefully, "What if we make her a part of the Tree of Life on the hillock in the center of the meadow? The celebration mainly takes place in the shade of the tree and she would be able to see the activities of the celebration and everyone would think it was just the same tree that had always been there. They would not know that Madison was there as a part of it. Because the Tree of Life is large, even much larger than she is, there would be no surprise to scare the people and no suspicion from them."

Looking at his wife excitedly the king said, "I think you might be right. It just might work. What do you think Lucky?" The king inquired of the silent leprechaun, "Do you think we can make this work?"

"Your highness," Lucky began, standing tall to speak to the king but still looking up at his face, "I do not possess your wisdom but if you can make her part of the Tree of Life I don't think anyone would know the difference and she could truly experience the celebration because, like the queen said, most of the celebration is held at the base of the tree. I agree with you about shrinking her, that is far too risky, and removing the enchantment for the entire celebration is not a good idea at all. First and foremost, we must protect everyone in our community as well as Madison."

"What do you think Madison?" the King asked turning to Madison. "We have to protect everyone during the celebration like you said. Would you like to attend the celebration as a part of the Tree of Life?" Smiling brightly with anticipation he looked up into Madison's youthfully beautiful face. "Even if the celebration did not happen, being part of a Tree of Life might be a worthwhile experience," the king coaxed gently, smiling up at her.

Giggling, Madison asked him, "Won't it be painful, being made part of a hard old tree?"

The king threw back his head and laughed. "Oh, Madison," he said between loud chuckles, "we would never do anything to hurt or harm you or the tree in any way. You see trees may feel hard to the touch but if you watch them you will see they are supple and bend with the wind, and the branches sway a little every time even the smallest bird lands on them. The leaves flutter in the breeze and the ones that flower are energized with sap that flows inside it to give life to the fruit they produce. Trees are not as hard as you might think. I think you might enjoy the experience a great deal. The other thing about a tree is the energy they exude, it is positive and restorative.

Our Tree of Life is a valuable part of our culture. Every kind of fruit, vegetable or flower that grows across our land starts from the seeds produced in this one very special tree. Every color of leaf and every type of tree originates as a part of the Tree of Life. When the seasons change the seeds formed from the flowers are blown across our land that go on to grow in the fields. After a time more flowers and trees begin growing from the seeds of the Tree of Life. We are most grateful for the bounty it gives to us."

Without hesitation Madison said excitedly, "Well, yes if you think it will be alright and do no harm; what do we do next?"

"Give us just a few minutes to think and talk about this before we proceed," the king said turning to his wife.

The king and queen walked a few feet away to talk between themselves to decide what would be the best way to accomplish this transformation for Madison and the Tree of Life.

"I think we should make Madison a part of the tree," the queen started. "Her body could be part of the trunk and her hair could be hidden like the moss and leafy branches that grow and hang long around the tree or simply hang down her back against the trunk. Her face can be part of the top of the tree and her eyes can look out of knots in the tree."

The king agreed, "It won't really feel odd to her as she will be supported as part of the tree. Ready Madison?" the king inquired turning to look at Madison. "I think we have it all figured out."

"Yes sir, I am," Madison said sounding confident while feeling a bit uncertain. Standing up she was ready to do whatever she was instructed to do and she faced the royal couple.

"We have a few things to do first," the king began to explain. "We must go to the Tree of Life and explain the plan. You see trees have feelings and we couldn't just insert you into the tree without letting it know you were coming and asking permission.

If the tree gives permission, then we will have to quickly remove the enchantment from the area and insert you inside of the tree. The tree must accept you and you must have a few moments to settle in to your new surroundings. Don't worry though the tree will protect you. Then we will replace the enchantment to protect our people and get the celebration started right on time."

"Your highnesses, I want to thank you very much for doing this for me," Madison said gratefully, "I understand this is extraordinarily generous and you do not usually do this because you must protect your people most of all. I feel very special to be allowed to have this experience and want to thank you both," looking from the king to the queen then to Lucky, "or all three of you I mean. I am sincerely grateful. Whenever you are ready I will be ready also."

CHAPTER 9

LIFTING THEIR HANDS IN UNISON the little King and Queen promptly disappeared without sound or motion.

"Where did they go?" Madison asked Lucky, turning completely around looking for the King and Queen. "What happened? Did I do something wrong?"

"They went to prepare everything like they said." Lucky explained. "Don't worry they will be back very soon."

Madison sat back down on the table. She hoped they wouldn't take very long. She was a little afraid, given enough time; they might change their minds and decide it was too much to ask. She had a scary thought – what if the tree said no? Could trees speak? She had never heard a tree speak. She had heard tree branches groan in the forest, but those weren't really words just noises made when branches moved against one another or the wind blew through them.

She thought about the trees in the forests near her home. They were very tall and had a clean smell of pine, cedar and earth. She was certain if she ever climbed to the top of one of the trees she would be able to see forever. The king had been right about one thing though, trees do bend and sway. She had seen that herself. The branches moved with the wind and the trunk of the tree moved also, but couldn't be seen so easily unless you were really watching for it. She had always felt that the gentle sway of the trees was a peaceful motion. She knew when she sat at the base of trees she was comforted by being there. Yes, she had to agree, the soothing, positive energy that a tree emitted was something to think about the next time she was in the forest. She knew she would appreciate the trees much more in the future.

The king and queen reappeared as suddenly as they had disappeared. "Are you ready?" they asked Madison smiling encouragingly up at her.

"Yes I am," she replied anxiously standing up smiling back at them. "Did the Tree of Life say it was okay for me to come?"

"Of course, otherwise we would not proceed," the king said confidently.

Twirling their hands toward the center of the meadow Madison could see a change in the air. It looked a little like swirling water that shimmered with iridescence. The air lightened and the breeze increased then Madison felt herself being gently lifted off of the ground toward an unknown destination. She leveled out with her feet behind her like she was flying with something holding her up in a flat position as though she were lying down on a soft comfortable cushion of air.

As she floated, she looked down and could see that indeed there was more to the meadow than she had been able to view before. She saw little doors and windows in front of rocky rolling hills covered in mossy grasses and she could see people moving around their small yards. There were roadways and animals. There were fields where she thought only grasses grew and could watch communities of people and how all of the things they needed in their lives were kept. She could see rows and rows of tables filled with food. She saw groups of people who seemed to be getting ready for something. She could feel the anticipation in the air. She realized, though she could see them, it was obvious they could not see her as they went along doing what they needed to do without fear. It was perfect; they were not afraid or aware of her presence at all. Looking ahead she could see a very large tree at the edge of the village whose high spreading branches were heavily leaved and flowered and were laden with fruit and vegetables of every kind. The proud tree appeared to stand guard over the entire area. As though she had done it many times before Madison felt herself being set carefully down on her feet in front of the tree.

"Madison," the king began, "turn your back to the tree and lean into it. You will feel the tree begin to embrace you. You will become part of the essence of nature. When our people look at the tree they will see only the bark and branches they have always seen, but within that matrix will be you. You won't actually be covered in bark but to all of the beings attending the celebration you will simply look like the tree. Most important of all is you must remain connected to the tree. You must always have a part of yourself touching the tree at all times. If you should lose touch the enchantment will be broken and every creature and person will be able to see you and I am certain they will flee in fear."

"I understand," Madison said in agreement, "I will keep a part of my body against the tree at all times. What if I have to move a little?"

The king said earnestly, "If you need to move around a little, do it slowly and deliberately. Think about a tree and how it gently sways with changes in temperature or wind; or, when a creature lands on it; it bends and dips with the weight regardless of how little weight the creature may actually have. The motion a tree makes is gentle and subtle; in fact, some beings who do not pay close attention to such things might think a tree does not move at all and is stiff and hard."

"Okay your highness, I understand. I can move but it has to be slowly and carefully in a tree like manner." Madison shook her head to the affirmative with understanding.

She turned her back to the large craggy trunk then backed up leaning into the bark. She felt as though she were being absorbed into the hard bark of the tree. She became part of the tree. She felt her arms reaching up into the branches and then a warm subtly pulsing feeling of life enveloped her. The King was right; the tree would really and truly protect her. She could actually feel it.

The old tree told Madison without speaking, just rest now; I will wake you at dawn so you can enjoy the celebration with everyone else.

As she began to drift off she wondered how the tree did that. She knew the tree didn't really talk to her, not in words anyway, but she clearly understood its message as though the tree had actually spoken out loud to her. It must be like the telepathy the king and queen communicated with. It was a great way to share a message as long as both parties could understand she admitted.

CHAPTER 10

"MADISON. MADISON. It's time to wake up." An unfamiliarly deep sounding voice said. "Come on Madison; you don't want to miss the party."

Opening her eyes from what seemed like a long dreamless sleep Madison felt herself stretch awake slowly. What was that warm yummy feeling around her, she wondered? It feels like the softness of her favorite blanket on her bed. With her eyes suddenly fluttering open Madison was awake. She quickly remembered where she was. She was a part of the Tree of Life and The Feast Day Festival celebration was about to begin. She was immediately excited. In her mind she thought, "Thank you for waking me," to the Tree.

"You are most welcome," the tree communicated. "Did you rest well?"

"I did rest well. I am very surprised that you feel soft and comforting rather than hard and barky like I thought you would feel."

"That is one of the most misunderstood things about trees." The Tree of Life happily explained. "Although trees have a rough exterior their inner core is softer and more malleable. The next time you are near a piece of wooden furniture that is smooth run your hands along its surface. You will find that the finish is as soft as cloth. Part of that reason is the person who made the furniture worked hard to make it feel that way. The other reason is if the wood were not soft on its own, nothing the woodworker could have done would make it smooth out, it would still be rough to the touch. Just try it and see."

"I will do that. We have a lot of different kinds of wood at my house."

"Look down." The tree said indicating the massive trunk where what looked like hundreds of beings of many types were gathering with food and tables and every kind of musical instrument from the finely crafted to what looked like handmade casual types. Small animals seemed to prance up the roads toward the tree with a gait of anticipation and excitement. Horses and cattle pulled carts and wagons filled with people and things she supposed would be needed for the celebration.

Young maidens and young men laughed and danced along the roadway with colorful streamers flying out behind their upheld hands. Each face was smiling and gleeful. Everyone was happy and seemed to be having fun even though the celebration hadn't officially begun.

As the carts and wagons approached walkers along the roadway the walkers stepped lively to the edge of the road to allow them to pass. People called out to one another in greeting and waved. The elderly people were offered a ride and room was made for them on the wagons and carts to transport them. Young healthy boys and girls were allowed to run alongside of the carts but it was obvious they didn't mind. They had to do something with all of that energy and happiness. Running was a good thing.

Madison curiously watched as long tables were set up then smaller round tables were scattered around in the shade of the tree. Little chairs seemed to magically appear around the tables and small centerpieces found their way to the tables. Where had all of that come from? What a lot of work it had to be for someone to make them.

The tree seemed to laugh a little at Madison's thoughts. He could understand that she would have no knowledge of how things happened in this unusual place. He explained to her that the fairies and pixies were the beings responsible for the centerpieces. He even said that the fairies that were tinkers were responsible for making some of the tables and the chairs made of metal.

Each kind of being and each individual person had a particular task they were responsible for. When each being, regardless of type, did what they were tasked with doing, everyone had everything they needed. From people who made things, or tended animals, to the animals that provided food to the people; each being had a purpose to provide something within the circle of life of the community."

Thinking about that Madison had to agree in her world it worked pretty much the same. In her family if her father did his job then others could do their job and so on and so on. If her mother did her job and helped people leaving the hospital with the equipment and help they needed when they got home, then others could care for them until they were better and could resume their own jobs and it would go on from there. Funny thing but it seemed so simple – until someone forgot what they were supposed to do or didn't want to do it.

Madison knew she had been guilty of failing to do her part at home sometimes. She could remember her mother and father asking her to do things but she really didn't want to right then, so she put it off. Then they would get upset because they had counted on her help then had to remind her or do it themselves. This meant whatever other thing Madison's parents needed to do would have to wait. Madison felt very badly that she had ever caused her parents to be upset.

"Madison," the Tree communicated, "this is The Feast Day Festival. While it is a day of celebration and joy it is also a day to reflect and learn. What have you learned from the thoughts you just had?"

Madison was surprised the tree read her thoughts, although she shouldn't have, they had been communicating for quite a while by then. "What I learned is that no one is ever alone and responsible for everything. Everyone is dependent on the help of someone else. In our homes we are dependent upon each other to see that the chores of the day are done. We also need each other for food so we can stay healthy. We need each other to share a word or thought, laughter and tears. We need to learn from each other too. I watch my mother and father and learn how men and women work together to take care of a family. I have seen them divide up tasks that need to be done. They also take special time for each of my sisters and me to meet whatever our needs are whether we need a smile, hug, help or direction. They also give us discipline if we start to stray in a direction they do not want us to go or would not be safe or healthy for us. If they are working on something and one of us needs them they stop what they are doing to help us they do. They are versatile that way." She thought smiling. "I understand so much better now."

"What good would a Tree of Life be if it couldn't help you learn and understand?"

CHAPTER 11

THE TREE SEEMED TO SWAY backward then lean slightly forward as the winds increased in force again. Madison bent with the tree in wonder. How could anyone think a tree was hard and straight and still, when it was so obvious they were flexible and could move? At the base of the center of the tree was a protrusion like platform that stood out from the bottom of the trunk. The winds seemed to gather and center on that place.

Two swirling clouds of differing colors flashed around and around in a shimmering kaleidoscope of transformation then slowly stilled and the shimmer lifted. As the air stilled, in its place, stood the King and Queen. Each held a long golden scepter in their hand that was topped with a clear ball that flashed every color brightly within its orb. It looked like lightening was trapped inside and fighting to get out.

Every eye was fixed on the royal couple in anticipation of their next action and words. Though everyone was silent the excitement could be felt as it pulsed through the crowd affecting everyone and everything.

The King raised his right hand holding the scepter and smiling said to the silent crowd, "Welcome friends. Today begins The Feast Day Festival. Today we gather together to celebrate life and prosperity. We will laugh and eat and dance and share a moment with each other in enjoyment of the day. Today we will renew ourselves for the coming year. We will ask questions of the wise and share knowledge with the young. We will express our love of each other and our land. Today is a day of renewal. After this day we will remember the kindnesses we give and the kindnesses given to us. We will remember the happiness and joy that is so very present in this celebration. Today we will play." With that said, the King and Queen raised their hands and scepters high. The orbs touched each other over their heads and the air ignited with color and excitement like a fireworks show finale. Smiling to the crowd the King announced in a booming voice, "Let The Feast Day Festival commence!"

Madison had never imagined a flurry of activity like she witnessed during The Feast Day Festival. Fairies and pixies flew up and down the tree, over and above the tables chasing or being chased by each other with the tiniest highly pitched giggles following their flight. Pixies plucked flowers and set them on tables then quickly disappeared only to show up again somewhere else with another bouquet. She was most surprised when the pixies and fairies actually landed on her and were unaware she was even there. She could hear them speaking to each other in tiny little voices about each other, the festival, and how much fun they were having. Then quick as a wink they would dash off flying to their next destination. Sooner or later Madison thought they might come back; after all she was part of the Tree of Life, which represented a safe haven to all of the beings before her, enjoying The Feast Day Festival.

The leprechauns made music and danced then they ate and drank and laughed and enjoyed the entire experience. They sought out others they had not seen in a while and enjoyed catching up with their activities, trials and successes since meeting them at the previous celebration.

Some of the leprechauns wore pointy hats and while they were dancing seemed to get so excited they flipped over and spun on the top of their hats like a spinning top toy. The leprechauns that had flat crowned hats would throw them on the ground and jump up on them and dance on the top making a thumping sound in time to the music. Every face had a smile. Every voice held joy. All eyes were happy. Joy, happiness and activity were the theme of the day that was for sure.

The big old tree seemed to gain strength from the positive energy exuded by him and surrounding him. She felt him being renewed just like the small beings at the base of the tree. It seemed like the tree took a long deep breath of satisfaction and pushed out what might be his chest. In doing so the tree gained strength and color. The fruit was a little bigger and more colorful. Blooms were a little brighter and fuller and more colorful. Leaves took on a deeper or brighter color as they gained in size. To Madison it was as though Mother Nature had come by the tree and painted everything just a little bit better than it had been before the celebration began. I guess that is what the King referred to when he said it was a time of renewal, Madison thought. She could see how everything and everyone appeared to be just a little bit more than they had been before the celebration began. Yes, like the Queen tried to explain to her, maybe it was possible to have a years' worth of fun in a single day. At the very least it looked like these people were trying to do so.

CHAPTER 12

AS THE DAY DANCED ON, Madison actually felt like she was a part of this unusual world. She watched the antics of the entertainers, dancers and magicians. She felt the love of laughing couples who walked hand in hand with eyes only for each other. She saw the happiness of anticipation when one person did something kind for another then waited to see how the action would be received and the delight when the effort was appreciated. Disappointment and unhappiness was not part of this day that was for certain. There seemed to be no anger or animosity. No negative energy at all.

So many ways to feel happy and positive; so many opportunities to make a difference in the lives of others; so many feelings she had not yet explored in her young life but would think about later. This day was filled with so much, so very much simple gladness.

As the sun crossed the sky and the day lengthened Madison could feel a subtle change in the atmosphere. The avid excitement of the daylight was replaced with a gradual softening. There were still people dancing and playing but it was changing.

In a flash she saw a large flame shoot up in the center of a nearby field then settle into a round fire like a fire pit.

"What is this?" Madison wondered.

"Just watch," the tree imparted to her gently. "Just watch."

CHAPTER 13

EVERY BEING MOVED TOWARD the fire; every eye watching in anticipation.

Little by little the sky darkened and the air smoothed. The breezes that had fluttered throughout the day seemed to calm to barely moving air - just a kiss of motion.

The fire seemed to gain strength from the calming of the area around it. All beings gathered around the fire were still and waited with unexpressed anticipation.

From the center of the flame, as though borne from the heat, materialized the King and Queen resplendent in clothes that seemed made of the finest golden thread. Each head crowned with gold they glowed in front of the fire as it danced a flaming background to them.

The kings voice could be clearly heard across the land. He said, "At the setting of the sun and the darkening of the skies begins the Time of Remembrance in The Feast Day Festival. This is the time we set aside to remember those who came before us and to think about those who will come after we have passed. It is also a time to reflect on who we are and what we have accomplished in the past year and what we hope to accomplish in future years. As important as what we want to be, is what we have been; for then and only then, will we learn from our triumphs and mistakes. In this time, we should look within ourselves and prepare for the next phase of our celebration."

If silence could be deepened it happened with the King's announcement. All activity stopped. Each being seemed to become calm and become somewhat trancelike. No one moved. They simply stayed right where they were. Slowly, one by one each person moved into a comfortable sitting or lying position upon the ground. Eyes gently closed. They looked like they were sleeping or at the very least resting. Young children cuddled up to their parents and drifted off.

"What's happening?" Madison asked the tree. "I don't understand this. It looks like everyone is taking a nap."

"You are partially right Madison," the Tree said. "In this part of the celebration, the Time of Remembrance, they are seeing in their minds where they came from and the people who helped teach them and make them into the people they are today. The people who have helped shape their lives. This reflection, or remembrance time, is important because we must never forget where we learned the lessons of life and who taught them to us. Whether the lessons are taught by thought, word or deed, each one is a particularly precious gift to the person upon whom they are given. It is up to the giver to decide whether they want to share or not with another particular being. Because they choose to share information with one special person is what makes the lesson precious. We must remember and be grateful."

"When will they wake up or begin whatever they do next?" Madison inquired of the tree.

"Patience Madison, patience." With that thought Madison felt herself drifting along and reflecting on her own life and those who had touched her with their lessons.

Flashes of her life were running through her mind. She was a tiny little girl looking up into the loving blue eyes of her Daddy while he held her above his head. He set her down on the floor and she crawled away as fast as she could on tiny little hands and knees laughing out loud. Daddy crawled right behind her and caught her in a hug. She squealed and laughed. Joy and laughter.

Softness and sleepiness. Madison squirmed into the fold of her mother's arm and surrendered to sleep. Her mother kissed the top of her head gently. Comfort. Safety. Love.

Feeling small in the corner of the couch she carefully read from a story book to her little sister.

Savannah watched the book and listened to little Madison read. Madison felt grown up to be able to share the story with Savannah. Helpful.

Madison looked down at Savannah and smiled. Savannah said, "I love it when you read to me. It makes every story special. Someday I want to read to you too." Humility. Gratitude.

Running for all she was worth as fast as she could go then flipping and flipping with her hands down on the floor then up in the air over and over again twisting and turning as she moved with her coach running along the sideline encouraging her to keep going. Then the order to stop with Madison making a perfect landing on her feet with her hands extended above her head and her back arched. The applause. The smile on her face; knowing she had done exactly as she had trained. The hug from her coach and teammates. Satisfaction at a job well done. Followed then by the cheers from her mother, father, sisters and friends letting her know she had done a great job. Strong, athletic and capable.

Why hadn't she just cleaned up her room and the playroom like her Daddy asked? She wanted to finish her picture not stop and clean things. She just didn't want to. Then when he asked her if she had done it she said yes, and told him a lie. Daddy was very upset when he found out. Madison was very upset that he found out before she could actually clean it so she would not have been telling a fib; or almost not telling a fib. She really didn't mean to stretch the truth; she just needed more time to finish. One of the hardest conversations she had ever had with her father came after she saw the sadness in her Daddy's eye when he realized her deception.

She remembered gathering up her courage and going to the garage where her father was working on a project. Cautiously she said, "Daddy can I talk to you about something?"

Turning to face his daughter he said, still sounding a little sad, "Sure. How can I help you?"

That's the way it always is she thought. Our parents are always ready to help us no matter how busy they are. Taking a deep breath, she began, "Daddy I am sorry I told you I had cleaned up my room when I hadn't even started it. I wanted to make you happy by saying I had done it because I knew if I told you I hadn't, you would be angry and disappointed in me and I never want to make you angry or disappoint you. In fact, I hoped you wouldn't go right away and check to see if it was done and I would have a chance to get it done before you noticed."

"Why didn't you clean your room when I asked?" he inquired.

"I had been thinking about an art project I wanted to work on for the past week and it all finally came together in my mind and I was working on it when you asked. I wanted to get the idea down before I forgot it. It isn't that I *wouldn't* clean my room I just *hadn't* done it yet when you asked." Madison admitted earnestly. "I love you Daddy and I am sorry I disappointed you. Can you forgive me Daddy?" Large tears streamed down Madison's face as she could no longer contain her emotions. She loved her Daddy so very much. She knew that she was feeling this way because of what she did and just wanted to fix it.

Kneeling down he took his eldest daughter in his arms and held her close. Her tears gave way to sobs and she cried the saddest tears of all. "Oh, Madison," her Daddy began with a thick sounding voice, "of course I forgive you. I don't ever want you to lie to me because it makes me feel that I cannot trust what you say. But when I told you to go clean your room I didn't take into consideration that you may have been busy with something that needed your attention right then. I am sorry that I did not consider that. Can you forgive *me*?" He asked smiling hopefully at her.

"I forgive you Daddy," Madison generously offered smiling through her tears.

"How about we make a deal?" Daddy asked hopefully, holding her away from him and looking her in the eye. "How about in the future, if I ask you to do something and you are working on a project that is important to you, you tell me that you are busy right then. I will ask you how long it will take and you can tell me that. Then we can come up with a time limit that works for us both. When the time is up, you can ask for more time and I can decide if what I need you to do can wait for more time."

Madison looked up at her father's kind face and said, "I think that will work Daddy. At least we can try. But Daddy, I think we need to consider what you are doing when we ask you to help us too. Sometimes you are in the middle of something and can't help right away either. You should be able to tell us that you need a few minutes before you help us also."

"You are right Madison; sometimes I do need a few minutes also. I think we need to talk to your Mom and see if this can be a family agreement. We can all be more considerate of each other," Daddy admitted, "let's go talk to your Mom about it and see what she says." Sadness, tears, sorrow, realization, understanding, compromise. Joy from sorrow. Confidence.

Savannah crying. "OMG not again," Madison heard herself saying angrily out loud. "You cry more than anyone, Savannah." Screaming even louder, her sister Savannah dashed from the playroom to the kitchen where their mother was cooking. Here we go Madison thought. Sure enough a few seconds later their mother filled the playroom doorway with an angry look on her face. "What, is going on in here?" Mother demanded. Madison began explaining that she was painting a picture on the stand up easel and had the paper side turned toward the light in the window so she could see better and Savannah wanted to write on the back, chalkboard side, with chalk, but that side was against the wall and she couldn't fit between them. "I told her I was almost finished and asked her to give me a few minutes. Then she started yelling that I better let her play or she was going to tell you - and here we are," Madison reflected.

Her Mother turned and called Savannah back into the room. Savannah continued to make a big deal out of her sister's refusal to let her use the back of the easel. Their Mother calmly said, "You girls have been fighting and squabbling between you for as long as you could both talk. I am telling you right now that you *MUST* find a way to get along. You must also find a way to be respectful of each other's needs. Understand, I do not mean that because you decide you want to use a toy or something that Madison is using," Mother said addressing Savannah directly, "Madison should just give it up to you because you want it. You need to see that she is working on a project and let her finish Savannah. But, Madison, you need to be flexible and grown up enough to tell Savannah that you need a few minutes then you can help her and let her play also.

Just remember girls, when all is said and done the one thing we have and can count on is our family. You are sisters and will always be sisters. With that comes responsibility and understanding. The sooner you figure it out and learn to get along the easier it will be to compromise and come to decisions that work for you both." With that their mother left the doorway and her daughters to figure things out between them. Understanding. Fairness. Patience. Compromise.

Reaching out Madison saw her hand grasping the tiny little hand of a new born baby. It was her littlest sister, Brooklyn. She was so tiny and cute. She looked up at Madison and seemed to know her. Madison's heart was filled with love for this tiny little person. There was so much Madison wanted to tell her; so much she had to teach her; so much to show her. Brooklyn had been born early and had to fight for her life their parents told them; she was a strong and brave little girl. Life was new with Brooklyn in it. Protection. Love. Generosity.

CHAPTER 14

"WATCH MADISON," THE TREE OF LIFE instructed bringing her to present time, "Look for the change."

As she watched the people seemed to become animated again. Slowly and surely as though waking up from a deep sleep they blinked, stretched, looked around them and reconnected with the world. They saw and acknowledged others nearby. They looked toward the flame seeking further instruction from the king and queen who were waiting.

Raising her tiny hands and in a clearly understood voice the queen said, "In this phase of our celebration we will recognize and display 'Gratitude' toward others for their kindnesses. Each one of us has been blessed by the kindness and deeds of others from the day we were born. Now is the time to give thanks and let others know that their gifts are appreciated no matter how large or small."

She turned and reached out her hands and curtseyed to the king. "With my undying gratitude I thank you for loving me unconditionally and making me your Queen."

The king bowed low to the queen then bent on one knee and said, "As I grew to a man I always hoped that someday, someway, I would be presented with the exactly perfect life partner with which to share my life and rule this kingdom. I never wanted someone who would always agree with me but someone who would challenge me to think beyond the ordinary and assist me to come to, not good, but great solutions to the problems I would face. I found that in you, my queen, and am an especially grateful and humble man."

Together they stood arms around each other's back, and faced the crowd. The king spoke, "we have expressed our gratitude to each other and now wish to express to each of you our gratitude and thanks in making this the most prosperous, healthy, and happy kingdom we could have ever imagined. Thank you. Thank you all. Now go forth and share your gratitude with to each other."

With that people young and old began milling around smiling and hugging each other. Shaking hands in greeting everyone seemed to speak at once. They couldn't wait to see the next person and express themselves. The noise level grew as each person spoke.

A little giggle escaped Madison making the branches on the Tree of Life flutter and bend. "What is so funny?" he inquired.

"Oh, I was just thinking that the people expressing their gratitude are a lot like me."

"What do you mean?" the Tree asked, puzzled. He couldn't think of anyway those people they were watching looked at all like Madison, who presently looked like a tree. Or even like her in her human form.

Madison picked up on the wise old trees thoughts. Oh, I didn't mean they physically *look* like me. I meant they are talking like me as fast as they can get the words out of their mouths. That's what my Mom says I do. She says I ask so many questions so fast no one has a second to think before they answer me. Then I ask so many they forget the questions and don't know what to answer first or last. I guess she is right too. I'm just afraid if I don't tell someone everything all at once I will get distracted and forget; so I take a deep breath and do it all at once.

Chuckling, the Tree of Life acknowledged Madison's statement. "In my years on earth, and there have been a considerable number, I have learned that time is not nearly as fleeting as we might think. Few things that you say are ever truly forgotten. When people have conversations they exchange information, almost like one side says their part and the other says their part. Then there is a period of time where one tries to convince the other they are right and the other tries to impart their thoughts and explain their feelings. In the inevitable end they either agree to agree; agree to disagree or walk away certain they are right and the other person is wrong but wouldn't listen. In any case, usually all of the issues are touched on and the subjects you might have wanted to comment on go by the wayside because they were not really important issues just minor topics that can be thought about and brought up again if they become more important later. Words have great power Madison, always remember this.

Madison had to agree with the Tree of Life. He was so wise. She was grateful to her parents for the many things they had already taught her and for what they would teach her and her sisters in the future.

Madison understood gratitude. She and her sisters were taught to be grateful in their home. She knew she didn't always appreciate it but she knew she should. Madison knew when she went home she would spend a lot of time thinking about this adventure and the lessons brought to her attention. She knew she would be more active in being grateful in the future. She also thought she would find a way to share this lesson with her younger sisters. Yes, that would be a good thing to do. She would probably even share this with her parents so they would know how grateful she was for all they taught her and for the lessons to come. She supposed she was even grateful for the lessons they stood back and let her learn on her own, even if they suspected she might be hurt along the way. That is when they stepped up in support of her, which was another lesson to be grateful for.

At the base of the Tree of Life the chatter and laughter reached a crescendo. Music began to play again and the people continued to thank each other. They danced. They drank. They ate. They laughed. Again, they shared the joy of The Feast Day Festival with each other. The men pounded each other on the back and the women hugged each other.

The Feast Day Festival was in full swing again. And on and on it went throughout the rest of the night. Madison watched and felt somehow empowered for this experience. Her heart was full. She had a positive energy about her she had never known before. She felt she understood life a little differently and would feel gratitude far more than she ever had in the past.

CHAPTER 15

THE STARS TWINKLED IN THE SKY as the night danced on and so did the people. Cheer was in every smile. True heartfelt happiness exuded from every one as the gentle night progressed.

Sunrise began with a gradual lightening of the sky. The atmosphere seemed to change a little as people became aware of the change. There was no rush to close up the tables and chairs or stop the celebration. No need to quit eating the delicious food or drink the variety of coffee, tea, ales, wines and waters. Children still laughed, ran and played.

"The sun is coming up," Madison quietly asked the Tree. "What will happen when it's daylight?"

"You sound sad Madison," the Tree said. "Are you sad?"

"Well not sad exactly," she admitted, "I have enjoyed this celebration so very much I just hate to see it come to an end. Also, I don't know what happens to the people when the celebration is over.

What does happen? Can you tell me? I really want to know. Will I be able to see the people?"

The Tree of Life listened carefully understanding her concern. He supposed he would feel the same if he hadn't been a part of a thousand episodes of The Feast Day Festival since he was a tiny sapling. In this case he did know how it all turned out. "Madison," he began, "since the beginning of time, the earth and people have taken time out of their busy schedules to celebrate. They celebrated the rising of the moon; the rising of the sun; the rising of the stars. They celebrated the changing of royalty. They celebrated births, deaths, birthdays, anniversaries, and long anticipated homecomings and weddings. Do you understand what part is the same about all of those celebrations?"

"Not really," Madison admitted frankly. "I don't understand what would be the same in celebrating all of those things except there is a celebration."

"Exactly." The Tree stated. "The common element to all of those occasions is celebration and the shared joy of every person attending those celebrations. You see, even with those celebrations that denote a sad time, like a death, there is still an element of joy in the fact that the person who died had first lived, loved and shared with others. So even in the saddest of times there are reasons to be happy."

"I'll have to think about that one for a while," Madison admitted seriously.

Shortly before the uppermost edge of the rising sun could crest the rounded hills in the distance, the fire died away, and the king and queen stepped upon the platform that was part of the Tree of Life. Holding hands and smiling down at the people gathered at the base they waited for the talking to quiet.

"With the sun's rise, The Feast Day Festival will end. With its ending will come the beginning of another year. Each of us will return to our jobs and continue to make certain our life's purpose is carried on for another year. It is important to say and understand that the jobs that we all do affect each and every other being in our kingdom either directly or indirectly. We touch each other because we cannot live or function without each other. Every person of every type contributes to the overall success of our kingdom. As you go through the chores of daily life remember that you are a vitally important piece of the bigger puzzle that makes all of this work. Also, as you go through the next year continue feeling grateful for your reflections today and let them guide you in the way you treat and are treated by others. When given a choice in how to face someone think of how you would want to be treated and go the gentle way. As the sun peaks up I invite you to rest today and ready yourself for tomorrow and a resumption of your life's purpose."

The crowd cheered and yelled. They thanked their king and queen for the wonderful Feast Day Festival and prepared to rest.

The king and queen turned on the platform and faced the Tree of Life. They asked if Madison had enjoyed the celebration.

She said, "Yes, yes, I did. Thank you so very much for making this experience possible. It was more than I ever could have imagined. I will never forget what I saw and what I learned. Most of all I will always be grateful to you and the people in my regular life who have reached out and given me help."

The King asked her solemnly, "Did watching the celebration answer the question you asked us?"

"Which question?" Madison asked, knowing she had probably asked dozens.

"The question of whether it was possible to gather a year's worth of fun in a single day?"

"Oh. That question," Madison acknowledged shyly. "I think they had a lot of fun in the past day, I know I did, just watching them. But I still think it is good to have fun every day. That is what I know so I would miss it if I only got to experience it one day a year. Your people don't know another way so I think they don't miss what they don't know. Does that make sense?"

"What you said makes perfect sense Madison." The little queen said smiling. "You have your fun in bits and pieces a little at a time. Our people have their fun all at once and let it nurture them all year. You are also correct that we do not know a different way, so are not affected by what we don't know."

Turning to her king the queen said, "It is good to get the opinions of others from time to time. It keeps us on track and thinking positively about what is best for the people."

"I agree," said the king. Turning to their guest, he added, "Thank you for your input and insight Madison." Reaching out he hugged his wife and apologized for having to leave stating he had pressing matters requiring his attention.

The queen hugged him back and said she would join him soon. She looked at the Tree of Life and asked if he were ready to release his new friend. The Tree indicted he was, but that he had not minded sharing the celebration with Madison at all. "She is a joyful companion," the Tree indicated.

"Very well," the Queen said. "When the people have all retired to their homes to rest we will quickly make the transition."

The queen turned quickly, hearing what sounded like someone running up behind her out of breath. She saw Lucky, red faced holding his stomach and breathing hard as he approached.

Breathlessly he asked, "Forgive me, my Queen, may I speak?" Bending at the waist he rested his hands on his knees before the Queen.

"Of course Lucky. How can I help you?"

"Well, I was just wondering if you were going to release Madison from the Tree of Life."

"Certainly I am," she stated. "The celebration is over and she must return to her home. Why do you ask?"

Standing up straight and adjusting his jacket he said, "I want to make sure she gets back to her home or wherever she started from. She must go to the place from which she came when she arrived here and I know the way. I would like to guide you, and her, back to that place."

"That is very kind of you Lucky." The queen stated gratefully, "Please stay and we will do that together."

Lucky was proud he could be of service to his queen. He had to fight being tired; after all, he had been up from dawn to dawn already and would have to wait awhile longer before he allowed himself to fully rest."

CHAPTER 16

"I JUST WANT TO KNOW if this is going to hurt." Madison asked bravely. "You can tell me. I can take it."

The queen looked at Madison with a smile and said, "Did it hurt to put you in the tree?"

"Well, no it didn't hurt to put me in here, but I don't know if it will hurt to take me out."

"It shouldn't hurt at all," the queen stated. "In fact you should feel very little at all."

"Ok. I'm ready. Let's go." Closing her eyes Madison gave in to the sensations around her. She could feel her body moving away from the comfort of the tree. The softness that had supported her within the tree gave way to cooling air as she was on her own again. She felt a flash as she was propelled upward. Opening her eyes she saw she was above the Tree of Life. "I will never forget you," she said earnestly, "thank you for the wisdom you shared with me, I am very grateful."

The Tree of Life seemed to bow toward her and smile. "I will never forget you either Madison. Safe travels wherever life takes you."

The queen indicated it was time to go and the three were magically and invisibly transported to where Madison's adventure in this new land began.

CHAPTER 17

LANDING SOFTLY ON HER FEET Madison could see she was indeed, right where she began this journey. Not where the pot of gold was, but where she began walking through the meadow when she first saw the rainbow across the valley. She saw the glow off in the distance. She could see the trees and flowers and the mossy grass that covered the open meadow areas and the butterflies that continued along their way changing colors while pollinating the flowers.

She looked at Lucky and said, "Thank you for coming to my room Lucky."

"Aw. I never said that was me," Lucky hedged shyly looking at his feet and twisting his body.

"I know it was you Lucky. I would know that red hair and green hat anywhere. I am grateful that you came to my home and somehow brought me to this magical and beautiful place. I will never forget you," she said earnestly bending to kiss him gently on the cheek.

Turning to the tiny little queen Madison said, "Your highness, you have given me the precious gift of experience. Not just experiencing The Feast Day Festival celebration but having the opportunity to share in its lessons by being part of the Tree of Life. I will never forget this day or you and King Jason. Generously, you let me witness the celebration while being a part of the Tree of Life. You also allowed me to learn from him. He is probably the worldliest wise being I will ever encounter. Just having had the opportunity to exchange ideas and listen to his opinions is invaluable. Please tell the king I am grateful to him also for allowing me to be at the celebration. I know that technically, I am the uninvitable but you invited me anyway and for that and so much more I sincerely thank you."

"Your thanks are appreciated Madison." The queen said, "What will be most important is how you use what you learned here and apply it in your daily life when you get home and have to deal with others. Remember sometimes the most important thing you can do is be patient with yourself and others you encounter along life's pathways."

Smiling the queen invited Madison to lie on a mound of soft grass. Madison fought back a yawn and did as the queen instructed. She felt for the coins in her pocket and then snuggled into the softness of the mossy grass. She rolled to her side with her knees drawn up. She *was* a little bit tired and could use a bit of rest. Sleepily her eyes closed and she felt herself drifting as though she were on a gently floating cloud.

CHAPTER 18

STIRRING SLEEPILY MADISON CAME awake on the floor of her bedroom. She was lying on the carpet with her head by the corner of the door. Something had changed though. She sat up abruptly pushing her hair out of her face trying to make sense of her thoughts. She remembered clearly the little leprechaun named Lucky and the pot of gold. She remembered the beautiful queen. She remembered the gently rolling green hills with the beautiful flowers of every kind and color. She remembered the king and the Tree of Life. She could still see and hear the sounds of The Feast Day Festival celebration. She remembered everything.

She stared at the corner of the doorframe and realized what was missing. Then she looked back around her room and found the plain off-white walls that she had been looking at earlier. There was no rainbow from one wall to another. There was no pot of gold by the doorframe either. There were no fairies circling the window. Where had it all gone she wondered? It was right over there in what seemed like, only a moment ago.

Her mother stepped to the doorway and said gently, "Hi sleepyhead, did you have a nice nap? You were resting so well I didn't want to disturb you by moving you up to the bed. It looked like you were having the nicest of dreams because every time I walked by you had a smile on your face. Do you remember what you dreamed about?"

"Oh Mom I have so much to tell you," Madison started excitedly sitting up on the floor, "I wasn't really here I was somewhere else."

"Really," Madison's mother said with surprise. Her eyes opened widely and her eyebrows rose, "you were right here every time I looked in on you. Where do you think you went?"

"Just listen to this," Madison began earnestly. She told her mother of finding herself in fields of green; so green it almost hurt your eyes to look at it; and the beautiful flowers and the tall trees. She told about the bees she heard and the color changing butterflies she saw that had fluttered around her like a wreath when she sat down. She explained about seeing the beautiful rainbow that turned into two rainbows one on top of the other. She said she wondered which side was the beginning of the rainbows and which side was the end. She said she saw a golden glow off in the distance and as she got closer, she chose that side to look for the pot of gold. She told her mother about hiding at the base of the dying tree and peaking around the bottom to see the actual pot of gold. She talked about her adventure until her voice was hoarse then took a deep breath and continued.

Half way through the conversation Madison's mother sat down on her bed and Madison climbed up next to her. They looked into each other's eyes and Madison continued. She told of a little man named Lucky, no bigger than a child, with a bench and stool and tiny tools and the twelve pair of shoes he made. She laughed when she told her mother Lucky thought she had exploded when she sneezed, then he *poofed* and disappeared. She said she had a lengthy conversation with him after he wasn't afraid of her anymore. She told about Lucky and the leprechauns living in enchanted houses in the hills that could not be seen by people like her. She told about The Feast Day Festival celebration and the king and queen, who, she remembered, had the same names as her parents Jason and Amanda. She thought it was funny she hadn't thought of that before. She told her mother that there really were fairies, gnomes, pixies, and sprites and of course there were leprechauns as she had just had a lengthy conversation with one and seen and listened to the others.

Madison explained about the Queen materializing in front of her. She told her mother she wasn't completely sure if the queen was a leprechaun, a fairy, a sprite, a gnome, a pixie or some combination of all of them but she was the most beautiful person she had ever seen. She told her mother that the queen looked like her.

Flattered, Madison's mother said thank you for the compliment, though she was almost certain Madison didn't realize she had given her one.

Madison went on to tell her mother that the queen seemed to know her. She seemed to know things about her and be able to see who she would become when she was grown up. "She wasn't like anyone I have ever known or met before," Madison admitted thoughtfully.

"Well that sounds like a mighty fine dream you had Madison," her mother said gently. "I am not sure if I have ever remembered a dream so vividly."

"That's because it wasn't a dream. It was for real Mom," Madison insisted earnestly looking directly into her mother's eyes. "I am telling the truth. You have to believe me; I would never lie to you."

"Wait! Hold on a minute! I can prove it!" Madison exclaimed remembering. Reaching deep into the pocket of her pants Madison withdrew a tiny black cloth bag. Inside were three slightly tarnished gold coins. "See Mom, here is my proof. The Queen gave these to me to remember my time with them. She gave me three so I could share the story of my adventure with Savannah and Brooklyn and give the other two coins to them."

Madison's mother looked down at the coins and Madison put them in her hand. Sure enough they looked like gold coins that had begun to slightly tarnish and they had weight and were plenty real.

She looked at her daughter and shook her head in admission. "I would never presume to know everything Madison. I don't believe just because I have never had a particular experience, the experiences of others are untrue. I feel that we all have a path we are destined to follow and in following those paths we will see and experience things that may never be seen or experienced by anyone else. Why they happen to some and not others will have to remain a mystery. You have the coins and memories to prove you had an adventure and I won't say or do anything to make you feel you did not have them. It is my hope that you will share your experiences in the land of the leprechauns, gnomes, sprites and fairies, with others and they will be encouraged to seek their own adventures. I'm just glad you made it back safely to us because we love you very much."

Madison reached out and hugged her mother so she could bask in the warmth of the love she received from her. There was no one like her Mom, she was very special indeed; whether she was right here at home, or she was the tiny queen of the Leprechauns in the green Irish land where Lucky lives.

THE   END

ABOUT THE AUTHOR

Hello Readers,

Thank you for taking the time to read my first published book. It has been my lifelong dream to write and publish meaningful stories to entertain the young and mature at heart. This story began as a gift for my great-niece for her 9th birthday. After sharing it with her and her sisters it didn't take long for me to feel there could be more to the story. I continued doing research and was soon hooked. I continued to edit and add to the story off and on for two years until it became what you have read. It surprised me that adults enjoy this book as much as the children. Who knew?

I hope it brought a smile to your heart and made you remember how fun it could be to learn new things about faraway lands, their culture and folklore.

Through the Kindle Publishing/CreateSpace programs I have been given a gift that helped to fulfill an aspiration I have had on my bucket list for decades. I am speechless with gratitude.

From my country home in Southern Nevada I continue to let my imagination go wild. Look for more stories to come. I live with an old grumpy dachshund and my sister.

Please go to the site where you purchased this book and leave me a review. There is no better advertisement than word of mouth and in this way you can share with me and others.

Happy reading,
V. L. Simer